RACE INTO THE PAST

Megan Stine and H. William Stine

ILLUSTRATIONS BY DAVID G. KLEIN

SCHOLASTIC INC.
New York Toronto London Auckland Sydney Tokyo

For Lew,
who almost drove at Indianapolis,
and Mike,
who would have won if she ever had

ISBN 0-590-32868-9

12 11 10 9 8 7 6 5 4 3 2 1   1   4 5 6 7 8/8

BEWARE!!!
DO NOT READ THIS BOOK FROM BEGINNING TO END

Y ou are about to take a ride in a race car that is so fast it will send you backwards on a trip through time. And when your head stops spinning, you'll find yourself in a very *different* kind of race, in a very *different* time — 1915!

There is a whole life waiting for you back there — perhaps it really is *your* previous life! In any event, it is filled with danger and intrigue, and *you* must make the decisions that determine whether you win or lose, live or die!

Follow the instructions at the bottom of each page and choose the paths that take you where you want to go. But be careful — there are hidden dangers at every curve in the road! If you make the right choices, you can win not only the race, but fame and glory as well. But the wrong choices can lead you to an adventure you'll wish you never had!

Now fasten your seatbelt and hold on tight. Here goes!

Turn to PAGE 2.

"Don't ever, ever, ever tell your parents I let you do this," your Uncle Matt says to you as he fastens the crash helmet under your chin. The two of you are sausaged bobsled style into his million-dollar custom-built race car, sitting smack out in the middle of the Utah salt flats. As far as you look in any direction, all you can see is open space — flat, black-and-white, cracked earth.

"All set?" your Uncle Matt asks. You can barely hear your uncle's voice over the roar of the enormous engine. You can barely move because the steering wheel is pinned against your ribs, and you can barely breathe from the combination of the thin Utah air and your racing heart. But it doesn't matter, because this is the moment you've been begging for — a chance to feel what it's like to break the speed of sound in a car built by your favorite person in the whole world.

Without waiting for an answer from you, your uncle gives a signal, and the two mechanics move out of the way. And BAM! You're up to 100 mph in seconds. The force is unbelievably strong, more than you imagined, and so far you're only going 248 mph. The world is whipping by you in a gray blur.

Go on to PAGE 3.

Suddenly, the strangest feeling overcomes you — the feeling that you've been here before. But that's impossible, isn't it?

The G-force hits you like a boxing glove, and for a second you close your eyes and think you feel the car slow down to a crawl. When you open your eyes you're not in your Uncle Matt's race car at all. You're sitting next to a man who's wearing a long white coat and old-fashioned aviator's helmet and goggles. And he's driving a bulky metal race car that looks like an antique. He looks over at you and smiles. "I'm going to win this race," he says. "I'm going to go down in history as the fastest man in the world in 1915."

1915??? Slowly your feeling begins to make a crazy kind of sense. Another life . . . another time. You *have* been here before. But what are you doing here now??!!

If you think it's possible that you've had another life in an earlier time, go on to PAGE 5.

If you don't believe in time travel and you think the idea of an earlier life totally impossible, swap this book with someone and go alphabetize the things in your closet!

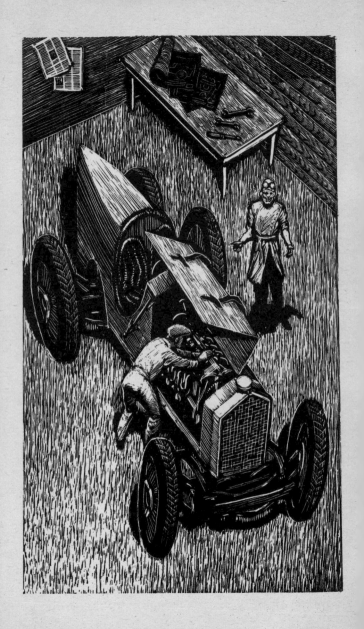

The old car bounces you down a dusty unpaved road at top speed — 90 mph — until you arrive at a warehouse that has been converted into a big garage. There are five other vintage 1915 race cars there, parked under a huge banner that says: 1915 CROSS-COUNTRY SPEED RACE OFFICIAL STARTING LINE. As soon as you pull up, a man in mechanic's coveralls lifts the hood and starts working on the engine.

You haven't said a word to the strange driver, but now he turns to you. "Jamie, I know you're still mad at me, but I can't take you with me on the race. I've got to take Corney. He helped me build this car and knows every nut and bolt of it. Besides that, it's going to be very dangerous. Baron von Furlhoofen will stop at nothing to win."

"Just remember who gave me *this*," the mechanic says, stamping his left foot, which isn't a real foot, but a wooden one. "You listen to your Uncle Max."

Uncle Max? Corney?? Jamie??? Your head is swimming with names you've never heard before and faces you've never seen. You walk away and into the garage. On the wall, there are blueprints of engines and cars, and newspaper clippings, and photographs showing the young daredevil race driver, Max Blunt, and his mechanic, Cornwallis "Corney" Hardesty.

Go on to PAGE 6.

Then your mouth falls open when you see a photograph of *you*, smiling and sitting in the driver's seat of the old racer!

Underneath the photo of you is a recent newspaper article, which reads:

> For the past five weeks, Jamie Blunt has been visiting his uncle and guardian, famous racing car driver Max Blunt, who is readying his specially designed race car for the historic Cross-Country Speed Race. Each race car will carry a two-man team — a driver and a mechanic/navigator — and will follow a specific, charted route from Boston to San Francisco. It is estimated that no one can make this grueling journey in less than five weeks. But local hero Max Blunt and his long-time rival, Baron von Furlhoofen, both say their cars can accomplish the course in 28 days.

Suddenly, you realize that you're not alone in the garage. A tall man in a heavy, brown leather coat has been lurking in a corner. He turns to you on his way out with cold eyes that make you shiver, and he says, "Keep your mouth shut about what you saw."

Something tells you that man wasn't supposed to be there, so you go back outside. But before you can ask Uncle Max who he was, Corney launches into a description of the other drivers in the race.

Go on to PAGE 7.

"Armando Passada," Corney says pointing to a bright red racing car, "is a snake without a rattle. Some people say that he works for Baron von Furlhoofen."

A white race car is next. "That's Duane Haskell. Four men died in the last race he entered. Everyone said it was coincidence," says Corney, "but I'm not so sure."

Next, he points out a green car with white stripes and a white car with green stripes. These belong to the McDonald twins, Don and Donald. Their parents couldn't tell them apart, so they gave them the same names. "They're rich. Racing isn't in their blood — money is," Corney says. "Those aren't mechanics riding with them. They're butlers.

"And in that black car," Corney mutters, "is Baron von Furlhoofen." *It's the man in the brown leather coat!*

Suddenly a man fires a gun and yells, "Gentlemen, start your engines!" The race is on, and the drivers run for their cars. Everyone except Uncle Max.

"Can't leave without the photograph of Jamie. It's always brought me good luck," Uncle Max says, and he runs back into the garage. Suddenly, the garage explodes!

If you want to wait to see if your uncle from the past is all right, go to PAGE 10.

If you want to jump into the car and try to catch up with the suspicious man in the brown leather coat, go to PAGE 12.

Right? Wrong!!

Before you can climb onto the horse's back, it bucks you off with a quick flip of its arched back. You hit the ground with a thump and the horse towers over you, standing on its back legs and kicking at you with its front hooves. You roll to one side and then to the other to avoid the hooves, which fall like lead weights. It is almost a relief to you when strong, harsh hands grab you away from the horse. The mob has you in its clutches again.

"The fire's out of control. Let's get out of here," panicked voices cry. They tie your hands with ropes and drag you to jail.

Angry mobs don't give you a choice. Go directly to PAGE 26.

You chose the radiator, not the clutch, pal. A useful choice if you want to blow off a little steam, but not much help in shifting from third to fourth. Where is your mind? It's a good thing you're long on muscle, however, because you and Corney have to push the car 20 miles to the next city.

The townspeople watch your grand entrance with amusement. Someone in the crowd shouts, "I wouldn't trade that headache of yours for my oldest, tiredest horse." That gives you an idea.

"Yeah, but would you trade a pig for this radiator?" you ask.

"What am I going to do with a radiator?" the man says. "I don't own no racing car."

"But what am I going to do with the pig?" you say slyly. "Who wants to find out?"

"Okay, I'll trade you a pig for a radiator," one farmer says.

Next, you trade the pig for a bag of cornmeal and a bottle of ulcer medicine. The crowd grows a little larger. A woman tells you that the cook at the restaurant has an ulcer, "probably from eating his own food." So you, Corney, and the crowd go over to the restaurant, where you trade the bag of cornmeal and the bottle of ulcer medicine for five free meals. Finally, you trade the five free meals for a new clutch.

Go on to PAGE 39.

As you run for the garage, you forget about Uncle Matt and his rocket-powered car and about your life 70 years in the future. Now the only thing in your mind is Uncle Max and that man in the brown leather coat. Uncle Max is badly hurt and burned, but he's still conscious. When you tell him about the man in the leather coat, he looks up at you and says, "Von Furlhoofen. He's fixed this race, too."

"We'll get him next time," Corney says.

"No! We've got to get him now and make him pay for what he's done," you say.

Uncle Max smiles at you. "I hoped you'd feel that way, Jamie. The two of you can win this race and catch him. I know it!

"There are three things you must know to win this race," Max says. "Von Furlhoofen has a glass right eye. If you want to sneak up on him or pass him, always do it on the right side. Second, never follow close behind his black car. I think he can propel a lethal gas from his exhaust pipe. And finally, *always* listen to Corney when he thinks something on the car needs to be fixed, but *never* listen to him when he's giving directions."

You and Corney run for the racer. As you slide behind the wheel, everything feels familiar to you and you think to yourself, I have been here before.

Go on to PAGE 14.

Left is right!! Er, uh . . . correct!! You pull yourself easily into the saddle, and the horse gallops away. Jamie Blunt must have been a very good rider, because everything feels smooth and natural to you as your horse leaps over burning fences. But the mob is still after you. The ones on foot you can outrun. And you guide the horse along the bumpiest paths to delay the cars and trucks. But the ones on horseback could catch up quickly if you make a mistake.

You gallop onto an old wooden bridge over a deep ravine and rein the horse in. Quickly, you leap out of the saddle. You've seen this trick in a dozen western movies. You slap the horse's rear flank to send it on as a decoy. The mob will chase the horse, while you hide in the latticework under the bridge.

But the horse doesn't move. You slap it again, but the horse still doesn't move.

Then you hear the voices and horse hooves coming over the hill and heading straight for the covered bridge. They'll be here in seconds.

If you want to jump off the bridge into the river 600 feet below, make the leap to PAGE 18.

If you still want to crawl under the bridge and hide in the latticework, go to PAGE 21.

Everyone is shouting and running except you. You don't know exactly what happened, but you know who is responsible. You walk directly to Uncle Max's car, pull a lever on the steering column, and then jump down and start turning the engine over with a metal hand crank. *What am I doing?* you think to yourself. You've never crank-started a car before, but it must be something that Jamie Blunt is very familiar with. You jump behind the wheel. Corney runs out of the garage and hops in, too.

"How is my uncle?" you ask, gripping the steering wheel tighter.

"Only a few broken bones. Baron von Furlhoofen must be losing his touch," Corney says, looking down at his wooden foot.

"What happened to your foot, Corney?"

"You ask me that all the time," Corney says. "Von Furlhoofen tried to bribe me to work for him to design and build his race car. But I said I liked working for your uncle. Late one night when I was working in the garage under this car all by myself, the car came crashing down off its jack. Everyone said it was a freak accident. But I know I heard the Baron in the garage—laughing."

"I'm going to get him, Corney. *I* know things no one else knows," you say, and your eyes watch the road for the black car and the brown leather coat of the Baron.

Go on to PAGE 13.

Corney directs you to stop in the next town in front of Wade Wilson's Garage.

"Now, Jamie, look carefully at the window over there with the four panes of glass. Three of them are real glass; one of them is empty. You've got to throw this wrench through the empty one. It's sort of a good luck tradition," Corney explains.

From this long distance all four panes look alike to you. But you throw the wrench, and it sails silently through the empty pane, falling with a clunk on the floor inside the garage. The crowd nearby reacts with happy applause . . . until someone says, "Hey look! That's the one! That's the kid. That's the one the police want."

"There must be a mistake," you shout, backing up. They grab you and drag you under the light of a gas streetlamp and compare you with a poster that says: WANTED FOR ARSON. $1000 REWARD. DANGEROUS YOUTH BURNED DOWN SCHOOL. USE FORCE IF NECESSARY.

"It's a mistake!" you keep shouting.

Just then a small explosion startles the mob. Corney has gotten the car to backfire, and in the confusion you are able to break free, leap into the car, and speed away.

If you want to take the route that goes back to the race, turn to PAGE 56.

If you want to take the quickest way out of town, turn to PAGE 22.

"We're catching up with them!" you shout as you see the pack of other racers in the distance.

"You don't know half the things this car can do!" Corney says.

As you pull up beside each racer, you're looking for the man in the brown leather coat. You pass Armando Passada, then Duane Haskell, then the McDonald twins (they seem to be having tea!).

But one car is missing from the pack — a black one with a driver wearing a brown leather coat. Where is Baron von Furlhoofen? You drive on, and finally — although you can hardly believe your eyes — you see the Baron's car abandoned along the side of the road! It's empty, and the Baron is nowhere around.

If you want to sabotage the Baron's car, go to PAGE 37.

If you want to wait for him to come back so you can confront him about the explosion, turn to PAGE 40.

If you just want to keep going to win the race, go to PAGE 43.

Corney checks and rechecks the car bit by bit, but he can't find any evidence that the Baron has tampered with your car.

"I told you," you can't help saying to Corney.

"Hold on — what's this?" Corney asks, tapping a small metal container.

Suddenly there is a small *pop!*, and the air turns green. Corney pulls himself out from under the car as fast as he can. He's on his feet, choking and clutching his throat. "Poison gas," is all he can sputter before he falls like a redwood, straight and stiff. The rumor Uncle Max told you is true, you think. The Baron can propel lethal gas. But not from his car — from yours! Your nose and throat and chest are burning as you fall to the ground next to Corney.

THE END

Matt and Corney work for half a day on the car. It's pretty clear that Corney doesn't like to take orders about his own car. But it's also clear that Corney is amazed at what Matt can do. The car looks pretty much the same on the outside, except that the boxiness has been rounded off. Front and rear spoilers are added to make the car more aerodynamic, so air will slide over the car instead of pushing against it. Under the hood is a crazy mixture of 1980s technology and 1915 parts and wires.

"This can-opener is almost ready to fly," Matt says finally.

"Yeah, but is it going to fly apart?" you ask.

"Some questions are better not asked," Corney says, tossing your Uncle Matt a rag to wipe his hands.

The three of you look at each other, and then smile. Each of you is thinking, *Whatever happens now, it's going to be worth it.*

If you want to see the Baron's face when Uncle Matt roars past him at 300 mph, hop in the car and race to PAGE 31.

"Maybe we'd better get the police ourselves," you say. Corney agrees.

But out on the street, you find that your car is missing! You walk to the police station and enter, feeling like soggy bread.

"Officer, where have you been? You've got to arrest the Henry Blurks, senior and junior. They are going to kill President Wilson tomorrow when he comes to christen the USS *Hawthorne*—just as that pretty woman told you tonight," Corney says.

"No woman has been in this station tonight," the police officer says. "The Henry Blurks, senior and junior, are two of the wealthiest men in Baltimore. The USS *Hawthorne* was christened two years ago, and in fact, it's sailing for London again tonight. And President Wilson is home in the White House sleeping peacefully."

You drag Corney down to the docks. There, parked by the gangplank of the USS *Hawthorne*, is your race car. "We've been set up to get us out of the race!" you shout.

You and Corney rush onto the ship. You search everywhere for the mysterious woman. Then there is a loud, deep whistle blast, and the ship jerks under your feet. The two of you run to the gangplank, but it's too late. The ship is indeed sailing. That's when you see the woman, standing by your car on the dock, waving good-bye.

THE END

Obviously you've never seen *Butch Cassidy and the Sundance Kid.*

See, Butch and Sundance are ready to jump off the edge of a cliff into a river because someone wants to kill them. But Sundance won't jump, and finally he says to Butch, "I can't swim." To which Butch Cassidy replies, "Swim?! The *fall* will probably kill you!!"

What a mistake. The fall did kill you. You ought to see more movies, really you should. Too bad.

THE END

Of course, maybe you did see *Butch Cassidy* and you decided to jump because in the movie they jumped and survived. Okay, you can be alive again. Go start the story over. Bye-bye.

You've made the right decision to follow Rotten And Crummy Road to continue the race. The road takes you to Barberton, an official stopping place on the route. While Corney is tending to the racer, you receive a telegram: *Uncle Max near death. Asking for you and Corney. Come immediately. Sooner if possible. Dr. Lishnus.*

You show the telegram to Corney, and there is no reason for words. You both know that catching Baron von Furlhoofen will have to wait for another race. You drive immediately and nonstop to the hospital in Boston, in a race where Life and Death mean much more to you than they did before.

As the miles and hours creep by, you think about telephones, television, jet planes, computers — all the things that will make this trip easier in the future. 1915 is a very frustrating time to be alive, but it would be a worse time if your Uncle Max were dead.

When you finally make it to the hospital, the doctor says that Uncle Max is still hanging on, but just barely. He lost a lot of blood during the accident, he's not responding to medicine, and his blood is not replacing itself fast enough.

But maybe there's a way you can save him!

If you're 16 years old or if you could pass for 16, go to PAGE 30.

If not, turn to PAGE 58.

"Okay, go ahead and kill me," you shout bravely. "But I'm warning you: If you do, you'll be killing the greatest mind reader this country has ever seen!"

The words *mind reader* ripple through the crowd.

"First, I am going to write down a number on the back of this WANTED poster," you say. You write the number 1089 and fold the paper. "Now, I want someone to call out a three-digit number with no two digits the same," you say.

After a long pause, someone in the crowd calls out, "846!"

"Now reverse those numbers," you say.

"648!" the voice calls out.

"Subtract the smaller number from the larger one and what do you get?" you ask.

"198," he calls out.

"Now reverse those numbers and add the two together," you say.

"198 plus 891 . . . the answer's 1089."

"Now look at the number I've written on the poster," you say.

One by one at first, then in large groups, the people crowd around the poster, amazed at your ability. And while no one is looking, you sneak away, back to the racing car.

If you want to find out what happens to you during the race, go on to PAGE 50.

If you just want to know whether you win or lose, go to PAGE 90.

The horse hooves clattering onto the bridge sound like thunder. Finally the thunder stops, replaced by men's footsteps on the bridge.

"Here's the horse. Spread out, boys. We're close, real close," a voice says.

"Zeke, you take a couple of boys and crawl under the bridge. It's a lot easier to hide under there than it is to jump in the river."

You don't have much time left. Quickly, you take off your jacket. You wrap it around a large loose board under the bridge. When you hear the men begin to climb down under the bridge, you shout, "Don't come near me!" And then you push the board as hard as you can. The huge board, wearing your jacket, falls into the water below.

"Look at that!" a voice says. "The little fool jumped."

"Well," says a voice above you, "I guess the water will put out the little firebug."

Nighttime. Crickets and your heartbeat are all you can hear. You wait for hours to make sure the men have gone. Then you climb back on the bridge and run for the other side.

As you round a bend, you see a campfire crackling in the distance.

If you want to go toward it, go toward PAGE 33.

If you want to run away from it, run to PAGE 52.

You take side streets out of town and then follow some dirt roads until you come to a farmhouse with no lights in the window.

"What are we going to do?" you ask.

"They're coming after us. I see headlights and torches in the distance," Corney says. "I think we'd better find someplace to hide."

The farmhouse has an open garage, an open invitation for you and Corney. You turn the engine off and coast in as Corney quietly closes the garage door, just in time.

Suddenly the side door opens, and a lantern lights up one wall of the garage. (It's not like your garage at home. There are no bicycles or stacks of old newspapers. Instead, the shelves on the wall hold rows of glass jars with fruits and vegetables. An old gray-haired woman wearing a wool shawl is holding the lantern. Seeing you and Corney, she points a shotgun right at you. Her voice shakes, but her hand doesn't, as she says, "Tell me what you're doing here in no more than 10 words, or I'm personally sending you two up to heaven."

"I'm being chased for something I didn't do," you say carefully.

If you think she'll help you, go to PAGE 62.

If you think she won't, you obviously have no faith in human nature and are not the sort of person we want reading our books. Good-bye.

Too bad you're not a little more mathematically inclined because right now the odds are definitely against you. The mob quickly separates you from Corney. And as they sweep you away with them, their intentions become painfully clear. One of the townspeople shouts at you, "We've never had a lynching in this town before. But I think we'll get the *hang* of it real fast." Everyone laughs at the joke except you.

They are carrying you to the tallest tree in the county, which is even taller because it's at the top of a 300-foot cliff. 300 feet below is a shallow river that cannot conceal the jagged rocks of the riverbed.

"You can't hang me for something I didn't do!" you shout.

Struggling, with a strength from somewhere deep inside you, you break free of their clutching hands. You race to the top of the cliff; perhaps *this* is the race you were meant to win. You have only a second before they'll catch you. So you jump. The wind is pushing the skin back on your face — faster and harder. Then you black out.

Go on to PAGE 25.

When you wake up, you're stretched out on the backseat of your Uncle Matt's 10-year-old station wagon.

"What am I doing *here*?" you mutter, staring around you.

"I think you passed out in the car. I put you here," Uncle Matt says, pressing a cool, damp cloth to your forehead. "You didn't weigh *anything!* It was like you weren't even here."

You smile to yourself.

If you've had enough of the lynch mob and want to stay in the 1980s, go to PAGE 82.

If you want to go back to the past, turn to PAGE 34.

They throw you — literally — into a cell. You land on the bed, a wide wooden bench with a rat-eaten blanket on it.

"Welcome to the Pit," a voice says.

Once your eyes adjust to the blackness, you see that a man is looking at you from the adjoining cell. "My name is Howard '1-2-3' Cooper. I'm a bank robber. You've probably heard of me."

"No," you answer.

"No?! Were you born yesterday?"

"No, 70 years from now," you say.

"Not funny, kid. Now, listen: I've robbed every bank worth robbing east of Cleveland, Ohio, at least once. With me, robbing a bank is as easy as 1-2-3. That's how I got my nickname. What did you do?"

"Nothing," you say.

"Yeah, I believe that. And you think this is a hotel, right? I believe that, too," Howard Cooper says with a laugh. "Well, I'm checking out of this 'hotel' today. And if you help me, kid, I'll take you with me. Here's the plan: I'm going to pretend I'm sick, and you call the guard. The rest is up to me. Think about it, kid. Take your time. 1-2-3. Time's up. Are you going to help me escape, kid?"

If you want to try this escape plan, turn to PAGE 32.

If you don't want to be responsible for letting a dangerous bank robber loose, go to PAGE 36.

Armando's car bursts into flame on its last rollover. Corney shouts at you as your car roars away, "Armando wouldn't have wanted another driver's help. That's not the way race car drivers live . . . or die."

You don't say anything for another 30 minutes. Then your car starts grinding its gears, and Corney tells you to pull over immediately. "Maybe Armando knew what he was talking about," you say to Corney.

"Look — up ahead. It's the McDonald twins' cars!" you say.

"Well, good. Go up there and see if they have an extra clutch. If they don't, I'm afraid the race is over for us, Jamie," Corney says.

You run up the road to where the McDonald twins are sitting under a large beach umbrella. "Are you having car trouble?" you ask them.

"No, scones and marmalade," says Don. "Care to join us?"

"No, we need a clutch. Do you have one we could use?" you ask.

"What's a clutch?" ask the McDonalds.

"Don't you carry any spare parts for your racing cars?" you ask.

"Oh, if something breaks down, we usually just buy a new car. It's much easier that way," Donald says.

Turn to PAGE 28.

One of the McDonald twins' butlers, however, shows you a box with three spare parts and tells you to take what you need.

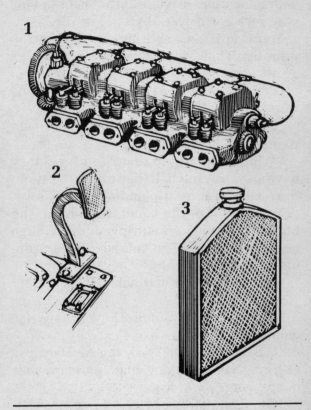

If you think No. 1 is the clutch, go to PAGE 64.

If you think No. 2 is the clutch, go to PAGE 39.

If you think No. 3 is the clutch, go to PAGE 9.

The streets of town are empty and silent. And the old guy with the haywagon starts to drive away as you and Corney cover every square inch of town looking for your racer.

Just then a green car with white stripes and a white car with green stripes pull into town. It's the McDonald twins.

"Hi-ho, pals," Don McDonald calls to you, climbing out of the green racer and waiting while his butler dusts off his driving suit.

"What's the name of this town? I think I'll buy it," Donald McDonald says.

"That's the third one today, sir," Donald's butler says.

"Look, guys, we need your help," you say. "Someone stole our racer. How about if I squeeze into one of your cars and Corncy squeezes into the other and you two help us look for our car?"

"I'm not sure our cars will hold enough," Don says.

"It's only for a few miles," you say.

"My brother meant we don't know if our cars will hold enough champagne for all of us," Donald explains.

Three towns, six hours, and two bottles of champagne later, you see your car. It's abandoned in a ditch — but fit as ever.

If you want to solve the mystery of how your car got there, turn to PAGE 89.

If you just want to go on with the race, go to PAGE 51.

"If he needs blood, give him a transfusion," you say. "I'll volunteer — maybe I'm the same blood type."

"Good heavens, child," the doctor sputters. "How do you know about such things? Why, the first practical method of blood transfusions was only discovered this year."

"I keep my ears open and I watch Carl Sagan," you snap, rolling up your sleeve.

Your blood types match. You are put in a bed next to Max's, tubes are inserted — in your arm and his — and strung between you. You look over at Uncle Max. He isn't moving . . . but suddenly the room starts revolving. Your vision gets blurry, so you think you'll close your eyes for a minute.

When you open your eyes, the fluorescent lights blind you at first, and the sound of the air conditioner in the window is loud and irritating. You're back in the 1980s.

"How did I get back? What happened?" you start to say. But it's not your turn to be asking questions, because there's someone in the bed next to you and he's scared.

"Where am I? What in heaven's name is going on, Jamie?" It's your Uncle Max!

"Uncle Max, this is going to sound a little off the wall, but you're in the 1980s now. But don't worry. Everything's going to be fine. In fact, I think you're really going to like it here."

THE END

You soon catch up with and pass the other cars in the race. They pull off the road, as though trying to avoid the path of a meteor.

Suddenly Corney pokes you in the side, and you pass it along to Uncle Matt, who's driving. There's a black car up ahead. You catch up quickly, and as Matt pulls the car alongside the Baron's racer, you wave politely. But . . . the Baron is not in the car!

Matt speeds past the racer a few miles and then pulls off the road sharply. You hide in the bushes and sit and watch the road. The black car soon drives by and it, too, pulls off the road. The driver quickly gets out of the car and runs away.

"That's it!" Matt says. "I just remembered something else I read about the Baron. He was accused by a number of competing drivers of planting fresh cars along the race trail," Matt explains.

"Well, then, let's nail him once and for all," you say. "I'm going to bring some photographers back here. When the Baron arrives, they'll get a picture of him with two cars!"

"No. Let's just go on and *win* the race!" Uncle Matt says. "That's the best and the surest way to get at him."

If you want to get the photographers, go to PAGE 81.

If you want to speed on ahead and make sure you win the race, go to PAGE 61.

"Guard! Guard!!" you shout at the top of your voice. "The guy in the next cell is really sick. He's lying on the floor!"

The guard, carrying a kerosene lantern, walks slowly down the rows of cells. Rats scatter from the light. He holds the light in front of Howard Cooper's cell. Cooper is lying on the floor, motionless. The guard unlocks the cell door and walks over to him. Cooper doesn't move. When the guard puts the lantern on the floor and leans over Howard Cooper, the struggle begins. It doesn't last very long. In seconds the guard is lying on the floor, motionless.

"You do good work, kid," Howard Cooper is saying, as he pockets the guard's pistol.

"I didn't think you were going to hurt him," you say. In the light of the lantern, you can see the guard's head is bleeding.

"Well, life is full of surprises, kid. And here's another one just for you: I'm leaving and you're staying," Howard Cooper says.

"We had a deal," you say.

"Only one of us believed that, kid. Look me up sometime when you're about 20 years smarter. So long, kid," Howard Cooper says, and then disappears into the darkness.

If you want to call for help for the bleeding, unconscious guard, go to PAGE 46.

If you want to reach through the bars and try to grab the keys on the floor, turn to PAGE 80.

A small figure, bundled in blankets, is crouching around the campfire.

"Could I have some soup?" you ask.

The pile of blankets moves, and a face looks up at you. It is *your* face—on another body! It's the real arsonist.

"They're looking for you," you say.

"Sounded to me like they were looking for *you*," the arsonist snaps back.

"Did you really do it? Did you really set fire to that school?" you ask.

"Yeah," the arsonist says with a smile. "I love fires. They burn the hate right out of you. Hey—I thought you wanted soup."

As you bend over the soup pot on the fire, the arsonist throws off the blankets. You see the club in his hand, but not soon enough to duck. You fall, holding your head.

You wake up the next day. The arsonist is gone; so are your clothes. You have to wear the arsonist's clothes, but you want to get rid of them as soon as you can.

In a small cornfield you quickly trade clothes with the scarecrow. Feeling a little safer in your new disguise, you walk the main roads and even hitchhike. In the fifth place you come to, you chop wood for a blacksmith. Your pay is 50 cents.

If you want to use the money to buy food, go to PAGE 42.

If you want to use it to telegraph Max, turn to PAGE 92.

"I *wasn't* here," you tell your Uncle Matt.

"Where were you?" he asks.

You're afraid he won't believe a word you say, but then you think of something that he will believe . . . if it's still there. You reach into your pocket and hand Matt a folded paper.

"This WANTED poster looks a lot like you. But it must be 60 years old," he says.

"70 years old, to be exact," you say. And then you begin to explain everything that happened. When you're done, Matt smiles, and you figure he's laughing at you.

"Baron von Furlhoofen was not one of the shining stars in the history of auto racing, I'll give you that," Uncle Matt says. "He was accused of a lot of things, but he was never caught at any of them. What makes you think you could beat him?"

"I could if you helped me," you say.

Now Uncle Matt looks serious.

"If you believe me this far, believe me one step further. Come back to the past with me, Uncle Matt," you say.

He looks at the WANTED poster and at you again and shakes his head a little. "Put your helmet on again and let's go get this creep once and for all!" he tells you.

Go on to PAGE 47.

"A jerk is a military courier, an undercover mailman," you quickly improvise. "You're one and so is my Uncle Max," you add quickly. You figure if he doesn't buy that story by the count of 5, your life will be over by the count of 10.

1, 2, 3, 4 . . .

"So you *know* your uncle is a spy?" the Baron says, unable to conceal his curiosity.

"Sure, he talks about it all the time—but only to me, of course. He trusts me and tells me everything," you say.

"What has he told you?" the Baron asks in a syrupy voice, patting you on the head.

"The first thing he told me was never talk with my hands and legs tied up . . . if you get my meaning, Baron," you say.

"You know many secrets?" the Baron asks, cutting the leather ties on your hands.

"I know things you couldn't begin to dream about," you say, with a sly smile.

"And I know just the person you should tell them to—Commander-Major Richtman," the Baron says, cutting the ties on your feet and pulling you out the door.

Are you still thinking quickly on your feet? If so, go to PAGE 72.

or

Is your heart pounding, are your hands sweating, is your mouth dry? You'd better close the book, because it's only going to get worse.

There's no way you'll help a lowlife like Howard Cooper.

"That's okay, kid. I can handle it myself. But don't ever say that old '1-2-3' never offered you anything," Howard Cooper says to you. He lies down on the floor of his cell and begins to call for the guard. "Guard! Hey, guard! Help!"

"What's all the racket in there?" a gruff voice calls through the darkness.

"Guard, one of these rats bit me. I'm sick— really sick," Howard Cooper moans.

"Just a minute. I'm coming," the guard calls back. "What's all the complaining?"

Before Cooper can say anything else, you yell, "Don't believe him! It's a trick. He's just trying to escape from jail."

The guard looks at you hard. "I know that," the guard says. "But we have to make this look real, don't we? Now, one more word out of you, kid, and I'll muzzle you for good."

The guard unlocks Howard Cooper's cell. He gives Howard his police revolver and says, "Okay, make it look like you'll kill me if anyone tries to stop you, Howard. We'll be out of here in no time.

They leave without waving good-bye.

Go to PAGE 46.

Even though you've only seen the Baron once and even though you've only been in 1915 a short time, the angry feeling in your stomach tells you you've taken up your Uncle Max's cause with a vengeance.

"Here's a present from my Uncle Max, Baron. I don't know him very well, but I'll bet he's five times the racer you are," you say as you stuff handful after handful of dirt into the Baron's gas tank. Maybe the Baron is too clever and you won't be able to prove that he blew up the garage and your uncle, but at least you can stop him from winning the race!

"That car will never start now," you tell Corney when you get back to your car.

"Too bad we won't be here to see the look on his face," Corney says.

Hours later, you stop in Horton, the first official fuel stop.

"You've got some catching up to do," the guy tells you as he fills your tank.

"You pump the gas; we'll do the driving," Corney says. "Sightseers," he mutters under his breath.

"Okay, say what you like," the guy answers, "but I'm telling you, there was a black racing car came through here an hour ago."

Go on to PAGE 38.

"How can that be?" you and Corney both say. You left the Baron's car miles behind you with dirt in the tank. You press on, sure that the gas station attendant has been inhaling too many fumes.

But just at dusk, when you're almost ready to stop and catch some sleep, you see the impossible—the Baron's car speeding along a half mile in front of you. He slows down until you pull alongside of him; then he salutes you formally and speeds off, leaving you and Corney with open mouths, choking on road dust.

Go on to PAGE 74.

Good work! You were able to come through in a clutch with the clutch! And now you're back on the road. You speed on for 16 days. You know it's 16 days because you stop 16 times to fix 16 flat tires.

However, in the middle of Nebraska, the road takes a surprising turn—it disappears entirely. They haven't built many roads this far west yet. There isn't even a wagon trail.

"What do we do now?" you ask Corney.

"Let's find a railroad track," Corney says.

You look at him as though he's lost his mind. It's against the rules of the race to take a train or to travel by anything except a car. But soon you see that Corney has something very different in mind. He places two boards as a ramp, then drives the car over the rail and onto the railroad ties. Soon, you are bumping down the tracks like the *Super Chief.*

A week later you're almost to the finish line on a real road. Suddenly you see the black racer of Baron von Furlhoofen!

As you begin gaining on the Baron's car, he begins shooting at your tires as a gesture of greeting. That's when you remember what your Uncle Max said about the Baron: He has a glass right eye!

Go to PAGE 60.

You drum your fingers nervously against the big black wooden steering wheel while Corney keeps opening and closing an allen wrench. There doesn't seem to be much to say as you lean on Von Furlhoofen's racer parked off the road. You're worried about your Uncle Max and hope that he's all right . . . but you're also remembering that you have another uncle, Uncle Matt, who must be worried about you.

"Good heavens! Where did she come from?" Corney asks.

You turn your head in the other direction and see a young woman, wearing a black coat over a long silk dress with sparkling pearls sewn on it, walking quickly up the gravel road toward you. She's obviously not from one of the nearby farms.

"There's going to be a murder," she says. "Please, you've got to help me stop it."

She soaks a corner of her lace handkerchief and dabs it against her dry lips. "Woodrow Wilson, the President of the United States," she says.

"Now, hold on there, Miss. How do you know someone is going to try to kill the President?" Corney asks.

"Because I was helping them. But I can't go through with it. They're looking for me; they want to kill me, too, but I don't care. We've got to save him," she says.

Go on to PAGE 41.

You haven't said anything because you've been trying to remember your American history. "No one ever tried to assassinate President Wilson," you say with a certainty that surprises both the young woman and Corney.

"No one has yet, you mean," the woman says. "But three days from now, in Baltimore, two men are going to try—my husband and my brother. And I'm the only one who can stop them."

"Baltimore is a four-day drive," Corney says, calculating his patriotism as well as the distances.

Maybe no one tried to assassinate Wilson because Jamie Blunt stopped them in 1915, you think to yourself. And maybe Jamie is more than just an important part of your history; maybe the name played an important role in American history, too. But how can you forget about the race and Uncle Max and the Baron?

If you want to help the woman, turn to PAGE 66.

If you don't want to, turn to PAGE 43.

Fifty cents doesn't seem like a lot of money to you, but in 1915 it can buy you a two-course dinner. The waiter even brings you a recent newspaper.

You're not having a bad time; and it's about time, after all you've been through. You sit there eating your dinner and reading your newspaper (but what's a newspaper without *Wizard of Id?*) until one of the headlines makes you jump up in surprise.

American Team Leads Cross-Country Race

The race car driving team of Cornwallis "Corney" Hardesty and young Jamie Blunt is nearing the finish line in San Francisco to conclude the Cross-Country Race of 1915. One contestant, the late Baron von Furlhoofen, a German driver, apparently lost his senses when his racer broke down and could not be fixed. He died of self-inflicted wounds.

The race may be concluded in the record time of 22 days.

But that can't be Jamie Blunt, because you're Jamie Blunt—at least, you are in this life. That has to be the arsonist, your double! You sit down quickly. You've got to get in touch with Uncle Max. He'll help you.

Then the second surprise hits you. Two little words will change your life forever: Food Poisoning! You and five other restaurant customers are dead within hours.

THE END

You drive on, leaving the Baron's empty car behind. You wonder what's happened to him. You hope it isn't anything pleasant. Corney tells you the next town is Otto's Corners. In most of the towns you passed through, people clustered on the sidewalks to cheer the drivers as the race cars zipped by. Flags waved, bands played, and children sat on their parents' shoulders to catch a quick glimpse of this historic event.

However, as you drive into Otto's Corners, there are no flags, no bands, no clusters of people. In fact, a large wagon full of hay is parked in the middle of Main Street.

"Would you move your wagon, please?" you ask the driver.

"Yeah," he says. "As soon as I'm ready. I'm not in any race, you know."

"Well, I am," you say.

Then you see something that interests you more than this discussion. It's a telegraph office. "Come on, Corney. I want to send a telegram to Uncle Max," you say, hopping out of the car. You and Corney send off a quick message to your uncle. When you return to Main Street the man is still there, and his wagon is still parked in the middle of the street—but your car is gone!

If you want to look around town for your car, go to PAGE 29.

If you suspect the old guy with the hay-wagon, turn to PAGE 54.

You get to Armando's car just in time to pull him and his co-driver out before the car catches fire. The co-driver is already dead. Armando looks at you through half-closed eyes and says again, "The Baron has tampered with all of the cars. Something terrible is going to happen to all of us." Those are his last words on the subject, his last words on any subject.

"I thought you said that some of the racers believed Armando worked for the Baron. Would the Baron do this to someone who works for him?" you ask. For some reason you're even a little angry at Corney. You can't believe that one of the racers has died.

"He would, Jamie; believe me, the Baron would stop at nothing," Corney says.

"Then let's go get the Baron," you say, jumping into the racer.

As you drive off, Corney says, "We'd better stop. If Armando is right, I've got to go over this car inch by inch and bolt by bolt, or we'll never finish the race, Jamie."

"The car's running perfectly, Corney. Let's make up some of the time we've lost," you say.

If you want to take Corney's advice, go to PAGE 15.

If you don't want to take his advice, go back to PAGE 10 and reread what Uncle Max told you.

You should have listened more closely to your Uncle Max's advice. Corney has steered you to a shortcut for getting lost. You wind your way up a road that ends at an iron gate. Beyond the gate is an enormous, dark mansion.

Just then the gate begins to creak open. You drive up to the mansion and look around the grounds. You find a World War I airplane, half-covered over with canvas tarps.

"Quite a view from here." Corney says. "Do you see what I see?"

You do. There in the distance is the Baron's black car speeding down the road. A few miles behind it is another black car—the one you poured dirt into.

"Two cars! the rotten cheater!" you exclaim. "Quick, Corney. Take the car and get back in the race. I'm going to find someone who can fly this plane. And I'll catch up with the Baron!"

As soon as Corney speeds off, a tall man steps out of the mansion, wearing an aviator's jacket, goggles, and a long white scarf. He walks straight to the airplane, and you follow him, explaining as you go that you have to catch up with a man in a black racer. The man nods and boosts you into the plane.

If you are afraid of heights, go to PAGE 71.

If you aren't, turn to PAGE 69.

So you did the right thing. So where did it get you? The townspeople hold the shortest trial in history in the morning and plan to hang you from the longest rope in the afternoon.

That afternoon the sun is shining, skies are translucent blue, and birds are singing. It's not exactly the kind of day you expected for your own hanging. The thick rope hugs your neck like a tight turtleneck sweater. The mayor gives a long speech, then turns to you and says, "Well, do you have any last words?"

You look around the town for a second, and then shout, "Look! Fire!"

The crowd turns and sees black smoke billowing out of the town hall building.

"There he goes," you shout, pointing at a short figure running at top speed. "That's the real arsonist!"

The crowd scatters. Minutes later, three strong men drag the young arsonist, who looks just like you, off to jail.

The people of the town ask if there's anything they can possibly do to make up for this terrible mistake they made. You say yes, you've always wanted a permanent place in history—you'd like it if they would rename their town after you.

They refuse.

THE END

Once again, just as you feel the *smack!* of breaking the sound barrier in Uncle Matt's rocket racer, the world slows to a crawl. You and Matt are transported back to 1915, back to the cross-country race.

"Jamie!" Corney shouts when you and Matt step out of the woods. "You're safe! How did you find me?"

"This man helped me," you say. "And he's going to help us, too."

But Corney isn't listening. Instead, he's watching Uncle Matt circle the old-time racer. "Keep away from that car. That's a complicated piece of machinery, mister," Corney warns.

"It's a can-opener," Uncle Matt says with a laugh, "but I can fix it."

"I said, keep away from my car," Corney says.

"Corney, listen," you say. "There's no time to explain, but Matt can help us beat the Baron. You want to do that, don't you?"

Uncle Matt raises the racer's hood. Suddenly Corney pulls a pistol from under his driving coveralls. "Touch one wire and I'll blow your head off," Corney says.

"Corney, listen to me. You're making a big mistake."

If you want to tell Corney you're from the future, turn to PAGE 63.

If you want to let Corney go and then try to get another car, turn to PAGE 68.

You drive straight ahead at top speed—90 miles an hour.

You never think of stopping, because sometimes as you round a curve or drive over a hill, you catch sight of an evil black racer with an equally evil driver, Baron von Furlhoofen.

But then, suddenly, your engine is on fire. You pull off the road and start throwing dirt on it as fast as you can. Once the fire is out Corney considers the damage.

"We'll be back on the road in no time at all," he says, ruffling your hair.

But "no time at all" isn't fast enough. At the back of the pack, you pull alongside one of the other racers. It's Armando Passada. His car suddenly veers into yours. You hit the brakes and pull away, but a second later his car sideswipes you again. Corney shakes his fist at Armando.

"I can't help it!" Armando says. "Something's wrong with my steering. The Baron tampered with my car—in fact, he's rigged all of the cars. Something terrible is going to happen to all of us." One second he's talking to you; the next second his car is rolling over and over onto its side, narrowly missing yours.

Do you stop to help Armando?

If you want to, go to PAGE 44.

If you don't want to help him, go to PAGE 27.

50

Here's what happens to you during the race:

• One of your wheels spins loose from the racer, and your out-of-control car barely misses hitting a bear straight on.

• A heavy rain in Arizona turns the roads to thick, sticky mud, and you get hit with a glob right in your open mouth.

• The Baron sets fire to a wooden covered bridge after he crosses it. You race across and make it.

• You take a nap.

• Corney takes a nap. Unfortunately, he's driving at the time.

• You approach San Francisco and the finish line is in sight. Suddenly, you feel like you could return to the 1980s if you could just get a little more speed out of the racer.

If you want to return to the future, floor it to PAGE 53.

If you'd like to stay in the past, put on the brakes, and try to stop on PAGE 78.

Resuming the race is a good idea, except, of course, there is one small glitch in the program—you're off the race route. However, you do have a map. To get back on track, you must take the road that goes southwest from where you are.

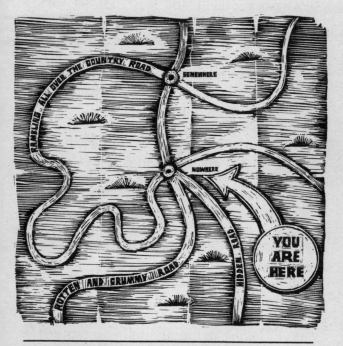

Decide which road you want to take, and count the number of letters in the name. That's the number of the PAGE you should turn to next. (Include the word ROAD when you count.)

If you take the wrong road, you will be out of the race and out of the story.

You follow the riverbank until it meets a railroad track. You hop on a freight car and ride for three cold days and nights. Finally the train stops in a town that is so small its bank is only robbed by midgets. But there is one welcome sight in this town. It's a banner that reads: WELCOME CROSS-COUNTRY RACING DRIVERS.

The next day all the racers roar through town, and Corney almost doesn't see you waving at him to stop. As you hop in the car, he can hardly believe it's you.

Who wins the race? The truth is, no one wins the race. The McDonald twins' cars break down, and they give up, settling for a quick purchase of half of Arizona for their summer home. Armando Passada's and Duane Haskell's cars don't make it through the Rocky Mountain snows. The Baron gets lost and makes quite a few enemies among a usually friendly tribe of Indians. And you and Corney drive your race car until the patches can't be patched anymore.

Corney is not totally discouraged, however. He's heard talk of some kind of crazy 500-mile race in Indianapolis. You smile the best you can, wondering what Corney and Uncle Max will *really* be doing during the First World War, which is coming faster than a speeding racer. At least you're together for now.

THE END

It works. You accelerate, faster and faster. The 1915 racer begins to disappear around you and the sleek, rocket-engine, experimental racer of your 1980s Uncle Matt forms around you. Once more you're squeezed into the right car, the right century, and between the strong arms of the right uncle. The exhilarating sensation of incredible speed is a secure feeling—that is, until your uncle's arms tense quickly around you, grabbing at the controls.

Something's wrong, you say to yourself. *I've come back just in time to crash and die!*

The rocket racer veers and brakes; the emergency parachute brakes flap behind you, slowing you even more until the million-dollar machine comes to a stop like a 50-cent toy with a dead D-battery.

There on the salt flats is a doe with a new fawn, wandering lost on very dangerous ground.

"I always brake for animals," Uncle Matt explains.

The first chance you get, you vow you'll buy him a bumper sticker to put on the racer.

THE END

You follow the haywagon out of town. The wagon driver must have something to hide, because he keeps stopping the wagon and listening for the sounds of someone following him. But he doesn't hear you.

About a mile out of town, he turns up a road leading to a farm. As he drives up the road, the barn door opens, and several men carrying lanterns step out, also checking the road for followers. As the haywagon goes in, they close the barn door behind them.

It takes you and Corney 15 minutes to get up to the barn on foot. Corney boosts you on his shoulders to an open window in the hayloft. You climb into the barn, trying not to rustle and snap the dry straw. You peer down to see the haywagon parked there, still filled with hay—and, you assume, your car! But the driver and the other men are gone. You jump down to open the door for Corney, and the two of you start digging at the hay on the wagon. But there's no car. Only hay and more hay.

"I guess we were wrong, Jamie," Corney says, trying to hide his anger. He hasn't lost just a car or a race. He's lost two years of his life, building that car.

But there's nothing to do but to go home and start building another race car for another race.

Go on to PAGE 55.

That race comes a year later. This time Corney and Uncle Max are squeezed into Corney's latest and fastest car. They are third in line on the starting line. Two cars away, in first position, is a new car driven by Baron von Furlhoofen. The official starter calls, "Gentlemen, start your engines," and the cars roar to life. Suddenly, you and Corney are staring at each other. The engine roar of the Baron's new car sounds totally familiar to you and to Corney. And now you know for sure what happened to your racer last year in the 1915 Cross-Country Race.

You walk over to the Baron and shake your head and say, "You don't have a chance. That's last year's model!"

THE END

As you speed through the darkness to get back on the open road, there are just as many people running after your car as there are people jumping out of its path. Corney is examining a copy of the WANTED poster and shaking his head in disbelief. "Wanted for arson . . . $1000 reward . . . burned down school . . . use force if necessary. If I didn't know you were you, Jamie, I'd think you were this kid. The drawing looks just like you," he says.

You smile to yourself and think, *If only you knew who I really am, Corney.* For a second your mind drifts from the road, and you remember your life in the 1980s and your Uncle Matt . . . years away and somehow not so important now, with your new Uncle Max somewhere between life and death and you on the trail of the man who did it.

But suddenly the road curves sharply left, and when you make the turn you run right smack into a four-car roadblock! With all your strength you yank the steering wheel to the right—where's power steering now that you really need it?—but a gunshot explodes one of your tires while your car is still on the edge of a dried-up field. In seconds you are surrounded by men with torches and rifles.

Go on to PAGE 57.

"Pull them out of there, boys," a man's voice orders.

Corney is out cold. His head hit the windshield when the car went into the spin. You're on your own, and from the looks of this crowd, you're pretty sure you won't have a chance to explain that you're innocent. You've got to act fast.

If you want to distract the men by knocking a torch out of someone's hand and starting a fire, go to PAGE 76.

If you want to stall for time, hoping Corney will wake up and help you get out of there, go to PAGE 84.

You volunteer to donate blood so that Max can have a transfusion, but the doctor says you're too young and that the modern transfusion techniques are too new.

"Doctor, you airhead, you are really a first-class drag!" you shout at him, slipping for the first time into language that feels more comfortable.

You rush out of the room, asking everyone you see to donate some of their blood for your uncle. But they've never heard of blood transfusions, and they don't like the idea at all!

"You know I'd do anything for him, Jamie," Corney says. "But I've got the wrong blood type. I can't help him."

He can't help Max, and no one else will, no matter how much you plead. And so Max slips away and dies.

Afterwards, you don't stay with Corney. You can't be with anyone. You don't feel you belong anywhere—especially in 1915 where people don't know enough about science and medicine to help a sick and dying man.

You spend the rest of your life traveling from city to city, country to country, looking for someone who can build a time machine. Because as far as you know, that's the only way to get out of this prison of the past and back to the future where you belong.

THE END

You and Corney follow the two men up the stairs. And soon you are in front of the door they entered and locked just seconds before. Room 1915—what else? There's no time to lose. You and Corney take a short running start and rush the door. It flies open under the weight of your shoulders.

"Don't move!" you shout. "Your little plan to kill the President isn't going to work."

"What are you talking about? Kill the President?" one of the men asks. "We sell straw hats."

"What a lie!" you say. You see two small black suitcases, just the right size for champagne bottles filled with nitroglycerin, on the floor under the beds. You drag them onto the beds, open them up, and discover that they're filled with . . . straw hats!

"Hey, Jamie, take a look at this," Corney says, throwing you a copy of today's newspaper.

"President Wilson's train arrives in Ames, Iowa. President to speak at meetings with farmers," you read slowly.

"It was all a trick!" Corney shouts, just as you hear your car engine start up. You run to the window and see the young woman behind the wheel, waving at you.

"Greetings from Baron von Furlhoofen," is all she says as she roars out of Baltimore with your racer.

THE END

"Pass him on the right!" you shout to Corney.

Corney doesn't ask for explanations. He steers to the right with all of his strength. The Baron turns his head farther around to see you out of his left eye.

"Stay to the right, Corney!" you shout.

Corney pulls the racer over even more. You're driving over bumps and small cactus plants. The Baron again raises his revolver at you, turning his head nearly all the way around to get a clear view of you with his one good eye.

Unfortunately, the Baron has taken his eye off the road a little too long, because he doesn't see the sudden curve coming up or the cliff beyond it—not until his car sails through the air and begins to plunge.

You and Corney arrive at the bottom of the cliff a few minutes after the crash.

"I can't find his body anywhere," you tell Corney. "The Baron must still be in his car."

"He's *not* in the car!" Corney tells you. "I don't know *how*, but he walked away from this crash."

But you are thinking that there is another explanation for the Baron's disappearance. Maybe that high-speed flight through the air was a slingshot that sent the Baron to another place in another time. *Where is he now and how does he like it?* you wonder.

THE END

You win the race, speeding past the finish line and the crowd of onlookers in a blur that stuns them into silence. No one on earth has seen a car travel that fast in 1915.

Quickly, you are swept away on the shoulders of the happy mob, until an explosion again stuns the crowd. Everyone turns to see your racer already half-eaten by an enormous hungry blaze. You and Corney rush over to Matt, who is standing near the blaze with his butane lighter.

"Why did you do that?" Corney asks, although he already knows the answer.

"Your victory belongs in 1915. That car doesn't," Matt says.

If you want to leave now and go on a triumphant world tour, turn to PAGE 77.

If you want to meet Corney's friend who says she's from the future, turn to PAGE 93.

Moving slowly and carefully, you hand the WANTED poster to the old woman. She looks at the poster, and then at you, and then at the poster again.

"So, there are two of you," she says.

"Yes," you say.

"But this one here is Jamie Blunt. Jamie's uncle is the world-famous racing car driver, Max Blunt," Corney says. "In fact, we're right in the middle of a race."

"A very convincing story," the woman says, "except for one detail. A day ago there was another child here with the same sad tale of being unjustly accused of a crime."

"But that was the real arsonist! The kid in the poster!" you say.

"Well, it looks like I have to make a choice, don't I?" the old woman says. "But I made up my mind yesterday. That poor child was telling the truth." Suddenly she fires her gun in the air. "I expect it'll take the sheriff about 60 seconds to get here."

The old woman was wrong about the arsonist, and she's wrong about the time. It takes them about 30 seconds to arrive and to clamp their hands on your arms, legs, and neck. Suddenly you get a bright idea—maybe your last. But can you pull it off?

If you are good at math, you just might be able to escape on PAGE 20.

If you're not good at math, go on to PAGE 24.

"Corney, listen to me. This is my Uncle Matt, and we're from the future. We live in the 1980s. We drove faster than the speed of sound in this rocket racer and somehow, when we did, we got tossed back 70 years. That's the short version of how we got here."

"That's the craziest thing I've ever heard of in my life," Corney says, not relaxing his trigger finger for an instant.

"Let me prove it. Let me do one thing to your car. If it doesn't convince you, then shoot," Uncle Matt says.

Matt tinkers and pounds and rearranges parts. After a few minutes he says, "Start her up." Corney gets behind the wheel as Matt cranks the engine. The engine bursts with new power, practically blowing the tailpipe off.

"What on earth did you do?" Corney asks.

"When it's done right, it's called turbocharging," Matt explains.

"I told you, Corney, we're from the future," you say, climbing into the car.

"You're the second person in my life to tell me that," Corney says. "The first one was a woman. Maybe I should have believed her, too."

"We'll talk about that on the way," Matt says. "Right now, we've got some driving to do, team."

"We've got to find the Baron," you say.

Go to PAGE 16.

You've made an interesting choice, selecting the overhead camshaft, because, as a matter of fact, in 1915 the overhead camshaft was a relatively new and exciting innovation on the racing circuit. However, it's also as far away from being a clutch as a pigeon is from being a bald eagle. And by the time you show your prize to Corney, who thinks you're playing a small but unfunny joke, the McDonald twins have concluded their light brunch and resumed the race. You're stuck out in the middle of nowhere with a dead car, a useless overhead camshaft, and an angry mechanic who doesn't have much more hair left to pull out.

Two days later, things get much worse. Corney has gone out of his mind, and you're pleading with him to come to his senses and stop trying to make a new clutch out of some twigs, a tin can lid, and a rabbit skin. But he's over the edge, ranting about opening a driving school for lizards right where you are.

If you ever get back to the future, you tell yourself, you'll learn your camshaft from your clutch. But that looks like a pretty big IF.

THE END

You're still at the wheel, hoping the road bumps and jumps will jar your memory about World War I. Von Furlhoofen . . . that name can curdle milk, but it doesn't ring a bell. *But there must have been a lot of German spies who went undetected in the United States at that time*, you think. And what better disguise could there be than that of an international race car driver? Sure—it would give him a reason to be in this country and to travel, transporting secret messages with him.

Two weeks later, as you're spinning out of a curve around a narrow mountain road, you see the black race car with the Baron at the wheel. He sees you, too, and speeds up. His car is no speed match for yours, and you begin to catch up with him on a bumpy straightaway. Suddenly his car starts spitting blue exhaust smoke. You hit the brake, remembering what Max said about the lethal gas from the Baron's car.

"Pass him! Pass him!" Corney shouts. "That's not gas! His car's breaking down."

You drive nonstop, passing two more duplicate Von Furlhoofen race cars. The next morning, you see a third.

If you suddenly think these race cars contain secret documents, stop and check this one out on PAGE 79.

If you think they don't, turn to PAGE 87.

On the way to Baltimore, the mysterious woman reveals the assassination plot.

"I love my husband and my brother. They are not bad men, but they could not resist $100,000. That is what they are being paid to kill the President. They do not know who is paying them or why these people want President Wilson murdered."

"Where do you fit in?" Corney asks.

"I wanted the money, too—until they finally told me how we were going to earn it," the woman says.

"How is it going to be done?" you ask.

"President Wilson is coming to Baltimore to christen a new ship, the USS *Hawthorne*. As usual, he will break a bottle of champagne on its bow. But it won't be champagne. The bottle will contain nitroglycerin," she explains.

The picture is vivid and gruesome. You floor the gas pedal and keep it there. If the race had been going to Baltimore, you would have won in record time.

"There they are—my brother and my husband," the woman says under her breath. She hides her face, as you follow the men to the steps of the Hotel Baltimore. "I'd better go for the police," she says.

If you want to wait outside for the police, go to PAGE 67.

If you want to follow them up to their room, go to PAGE 59.

It starts to rain as you wait outside the Hotel Baltimore for the police. An hour later, it's raining harder. Two hours later, you're still waiting.

You start to ask yourself certain questions. Why didn't the mysterious woman go to the police in the first place? If the assassins were in Baltimore, how was she helping them from 700 miles away in the middle of a cornfield? If she had been walking for a long time, why was her evening gown spotless? And why are you standing out here in the rain?

"Let's go in after them," you say.

You and Corney enter the Hotel Baltimore, looking like two walking sponges. "A couple of hours ago," you say to the desk clerk, "did a young man and an older man, both wearing brown suits with brown derby hats, come in here?"

"Yes, they most certainly did," the desk clerk says.

"Are they still here?" Corney asks. "They didn't slip out the back?"

"Why would they do that? You're talking about Mr. Henry Blurk and Mr. Henry Blurk, Jr. They're the owner and the manager of this hotel," the desk clerk says, holding out his hand for a tip.

"But did you know that they're *also* desperate killers?" Corney asks.

Go to PAGE 17.

Still pointing the gun at you, Corney gets into the car and drives off. But you and Uncle Matt are still determined to outrace the Baron, and nothing is going to stop you.

In a few hours another driver, Duane Haskell, speeds by, and you flag him down. He's losing, so he's not too particular about who fools with his car. Soon Uncle Matt has turned Haskell's heap into a hot rod.

Unfortunately, it's been a very hot afternoon, and you've all been sharing Haskell's canteen of water. 24 hours later, you all three are sharing something else—typhoid fever!

The next six weeks are a painful blur. You don't remember much. But one day the blur goes away, and you see Corney sitting by your bed.

"Uncle Matt?" you ask in a weak whisper. Corney just shakes his head no.

"You were pretty sick," Corney says. "Delirious. You kept telling people that you were from the future. You wanted to go to something called a Burger King. And you wanted to see Reggie Jackson play baseball again."

You drift off to sleep again. And you decide it won't be so bad living with Uncle Max and with Corney and driving their race cars. And maybe it won't be so hard to keep your secret to yourself . . . forever.

THE END

The pilot straps you tightly into the front seat of the old two-passenger plane. "This man you call a cheat and a murderer—do you know what I call him?" the pilot asks.

"What?" you shout above the roar of the engine as the propeller starts whirling.

"I call him my leader, a loyal soldier of Kaiser Wilhelm's proud German Army," the pilot shouts as the plane zips off the mountain runway into the dusky sky.

"Are you saying that Von Furlhoofen is working for the German Army? He's a World War I spy?" you shout.

"No, fool—he is a patriot and a hero! And the secret information he is carrying with him is too important to the German Army for a young troublemaker like you to get in his way," the pilot says.

You turn around to face him and see he is standing up and beginning to climb out of the plane. And your eyes fix on the parachute strapped to his back, something you neglected to ask for before the plane took off.

"Bon voyage, American fool!" the pilot calls out. Then he jumps from the plane.

If you want to survive this flight, you'd better hurry to PAGE 73.

The tall, silent pilot stands in front of the plane's propeller. He pushes it downward quickly, using all his muscle, and the prop begins to spin. The engine kicks over—but so does your stomach. You are so afraid of heights that you get dizzy, and you pass out immediately.

When you wake up, you expect to hear the roar of the airplane engine and feel the wind blowing against your face. But instead, it's quiet and you can't feel much of anything. You are tied up tighter than a mummy and propped against the wall inside a dark garage. As your eyes adjust, you recognize Baron von Furlhoofen's racer parked in the garage. The door opens, and the Baron and the pilot come in.

The Baron slaps you quickly and laughs. "You little fool! Do you think I care anything for this stupid race? This is all I care about," he says, waving a brown leather briefcase.

"Briefcases are a dime a dozen back where I come from," you say.

"But this is not!" he says, removing an envelope from the briefcase. "This is a secret document from the government of Kaiser Wilhelm. We Germans are urging Mexico to join with us in our glorious victory in this war. And when we win, we will generously reward our Mexican allies with Texas, New Mexico, and Arizona.

Go to PAGE 88.

The Baron was easy to bluff. Richtman is not so easy to fool. You have to dig deep into your memory of history to find something the Germans wanted to keep secret. But finally you think of it.

"What? How do you know we are planning to sink the ship the *Lusitania*? Only three people in all of Germany know about that plan!" the Commander-Major says.

"I don't like to reveal my sources. It's not professional," you say.

"How well can you withstand enormous pain, my young friend?" Richtman asks.

You look around the room. Richtman means business. You glare at the Baron. He got you into this mess, he practically killed your Uncle Max, and he's a German spy on top of everything else. There's no reason why you should be the only one to suffer in this situation.

"*He* told me the German secret," you say, pointing at the Baron.

It doesn't take Richtman very long to react to this information. He snaps his fingers and points to the Baron.

"I don't want anyone to ever find him," is all Richtman says as the five men drag the struggling Baron away.

When he's gone, Richtman turns again to you.

You're in big trouble. Hurry to PAGE 75.

You don't have time to watch the pilot's descent. The plane immediately begins to make its own rapid, spinning descent. Fortunately for you, you've seen a million old war movies on TV, so you've got a pretty good idea of what to do. You pull back on the stick, and the plane begins to right itself. You play with the controls until you know which does what, and then you look for a clear patch on the ground. Finally you bring the plane in for a very bumpy but safe landing.

John Wayne would be proud of you, kid.

"Hey, now. I thought you were flying up to catch the Baron," says the welcome voice of Corney.

"The guy who owned the plane wasn't a pilot. He was just giving me flying lessons," you say, jumping out of the plane and into the race car. For the next 24 hours, you don't stop for anything except gasoline.

"You're pushing the car too hard," Corney says.

You shake your head at him. Neither the car nor Corney knows how important it is to catch Von Furlhoofen now.

Maybe you can catch him on PAGE 65.

The dust clears in front of your windshield, but the fog doesn't clear from your mind. How did the Baron start a car that couldn't be started, and how could he get ahead of you once again?

Corney suddenly stands up as you speed along. He waves his fist at the disappearing black car and shouts, "If it's tricks you want, it's tricks you shall have, Baron!" Then Corney points toward a side road and shouts at you, "Turn here! We'll take a shortcut and get in front of him. I know these roads like the back of my hand!"

If you take Corney's advice, turn right to
PAGE 45.
If not, go straight ahead to PAGE 49.

"Let me break the news to you gently," you say. "I lied when I said the Baron was a double agent."

Richtman stamps his foot. "Then how," he says, "did you know about the *Lusitania*?"

"My history teacher told me, of course," you say. "The truth is, wartnose, I'm from the future. I live in the 1980s. And I know all kinds of secrets. I know that you're going to lose this war, but that won't stop you from starting another, which you'll also lose. I know that Americans are going to walk on the moon and take pictures of Venus. And we'll listen to miniature radios with headphones as we roller-skate across town."

The Commander-Major of the German Army is staring at you with all of the surprise and disbelief of a man who had just been spoken to by a radish. You begin to sing every Beatles song you know.

"You don't know anything!" Richtman shouts. "Get out of here!"

After you stop laughing, you leave the cabin and start to hitchhike. The first car that passes is a familiar race car with an equally familiar driver.

"Where have you been? Where's the Baron?" Corney asks.

"Forget about the Baron. He's out of the race—the human race!" you say, with some satisfaction.

THE END

An accused arsonist trying to start a fire—how smart is that? Quick thinking is not always the same as smart thinking, and this is a case in point. Not only does your act confirm the mob's belief that you're the arsonist, it also makes them really angry. Especially because you're successful at starting a fire that quickly engulfs a large portion of the field you're in.

The mob begins to shout: "Get the firebug. Get the firebug!" But you get free, and you run, push, and kick your way past all of the hands grabbing at you. The ground shakes under your feet. The mob can't decide whether to chase you or fight the fire. But you have only one goal in mind: *Escape!*

Finding Corney and the car is impossible. But suddenly you see your only chance. Someone in the mob has left a horse tied to the bumper of a truck.

"Over there!" someone shouts. "Get the firebug!"

There isn't a second to lose. You've got to steal the horse and ride off. Wait! Do you know how to ride a horse?

If you think you should mount a horse from the right side, go to PAGE 8.

If you think it's the left side, go to PAGE 11.

America in 1915 is happy to have three more heroes to cheer and celebrate. You, your Uncle Matt, and Corney have your own train car on a train that travels from San Francisco back to Boston, where the race began. In every city where the train stops, marching bands play.

In Boston, too, crowds cheer your arrival, but then Corney says good-bye. He's going to help Uncle Max recover from his injuries. Then they'll get busy on a new race car for next year. Maybe it won't go as fast as Uncle Matt's crazy racer, but it will take on the best racers 1916 will have to offer.

But you and Matt can't wait, and you sail across the Atlantic Ocean for London. It's a journey with a purpose — you hope that one of the great, imaginative science fiction writers or inventors can make a time machine to get you back to the 1980s. You meet H.G. Wells and several other brilliant people who are interested in the future.

Do you ever find someone to help you? There's only one way to know. If you're reading this in the 1980s, you made it! Congratulations!

THE END

You slow down just a little to avoid returning to the future. But Corney thinks you're nuts. He leans over and stomps on your gas-pedal foot and your car bolts across the finish line. You've won!

Like ants rushing toward a picnic, the people of San Francisco converge on you and Corney, shaking your hands and slapping your backs. The mood is jubilation itself . . . until a police officer slaps a pair of handcuffs on both of you.

"You're under arrest," the officer says.

"Wait a minute. The man you ought to arrest is Baron von Furlhoofen," you say.

"We'll get him, too," says the officer.

"You'd better, because he's the one who blew up my uncle!" you shout.

"I don't know anything about that. All I know is I've got orders to arrest anyone who crosses the finish line," the police officer says, reaching for a document in his pocket.

"Orders from whom?" Corney asks.

"Those two brothers — the McDonald twins. They knew they could never win the race, so they flew here and bought this land we're standing on right now."

"They bought the finish line?" you say.

"Yep, and you two are under arrest for trespassing on private property. Come on to jail quietly so I don't have to use force."

THE END

You search the car, but the Baron, as always, is way ahead of you. There *are* secrets hidden under the left front fender, but you never find them because a nitroglycerin booby trap explodes, blowing you and Corney to road dust.

However, when the authorities discover your abandoned car, they find in it a telegram you were planning to send to your Uncle Max. In it you explain that the Baron is a German spy. And although no proof is found, the accusation casts enough suspicion on him to force him to leave the country immediately — without the crucial documents he was after. And next year, Uncle Max builds a super race car, which he names the *Jamie Star.*

THE END

As you stretch your arm through the bars of your cell, the guard lifts his head and moans. You decide that he'll probably be okay, so you take the keys and run. You run right into Corney.

"Go on without me," you tell Corney. "If I stay with you, we'll always be taking back roads and looking over our shoulders. If you go alone, you've got a chance of beating the Baron for Max."

Corney finally agrees. He drives off, and you walk up the road to a nearby farmhouse.

"That's close enough," says a man holding a shotgun. "I didn't think you'd ever show your face around here again! I don't care if you *are* my one and only child — you're not welcome here."

"I'm not who you think I am," you say.

And the arsonist's father can see immediately that you're telling the truth.

He hides and protects you for the next two years. In the meantime you read in the paper that Corney *did* win the race, and Uncle Max was well enough to take the train to San Francisco to accept his part of the prize. Finally the real arsonist is caught, and now you're free to go. Although you really like the old man who's been hiding you, you can't resist going back to Max and Corney and the exciting life of racing that you were obviously meant to lead.

THE END

Uncle Matt may be partially right — but only partially. Winning the race would be a defeat for the Baron, but it wouldn't really pay him back for the deceit and treachery that are as natural to him as breathing. That's why you stuck to your guns about getting the photographers. And do you know what? *It works!*

Your idea actually achieves the impossible; it changes history! No longer will the Baron go down in the history books as someone who was only suspected or accused of crimes. The photographers bring reporters with them who dig and search and finally piece together enough evidence to lead to Von Furlhoofen's conviction for attempted murder against your uncle and five other racers, for defrauding racing organizations by using several cars in a race, and for attempting to bribe or blackmail other racers into dropping out of races.

The Baron is given a long prison sentence, so long, in fact, that he's still in jail when you are born about 60 years later.

THE END

Well, here you are back safe and sound in the world of artificial-colors-and-flavors-added. Back in the world where cars do not fall apart all the time; they're simply recalled. Behind you — 70 years ago — is the life-and-death struggle of your Uncle Max, the deadly rivalry between Baron von Furlhoofen and Corney, plus a very-eager-to-hang-you mob. And do you want to hurry back there and clear your name and win the race? Noooo way!!! You've had enough punishment and abuse for one car ride. You can't wait to get tied up in a traffic jam. In fact, the word gridlock is music to your ears.

"Let's go get a double carob-and-marshmallow sundae, Uncle Matt," you say when you're back on your feet.

"Well, I'm glad to see that breaking the sound barrier hasn't affected your stomach any," he says with a laugh. "Okay, let's get out of these racing suits and hop in my car and drive over."

"I'd rather walk," you say, ignoring the look he's giving you. "That way, I'll be sure of really getting there this year."

THE END

The rear-end crash sends the Baron and his car flying into the water, where there is a large splash and then a fiery explosion. But the impact sends you flying, too, and the ground begins to spin like a cassette suddenly going into fast-forward.

Everything gets black, and when the black clears away, you're looking up at your Uncle Matt in the 1980s.

"Don't take it so hard, kid. Everyone blacks out at the speed of sound the first time," Matt says to you. "But you're okay."

"Uncle Matt, have you ever heard of an old-time racer named Baron von Furlhoofen?" you ask.

Matt scratches his head. "Hey, you're going back even before my time, you know. But, yeah, there was a Von Furlhoofen racing shortly after the turn of the century. Weird guy. He died mysteriously in a cross-country race — 1915, I think. He was hit by another driver. The driver was never found; neither was the Baron. No one knew why the two of them were miles south of the finish area. Some people said Von Furlhoofen was a spy; others said he was just a bad driver."

"They're both right, Uncle Matt," you say.

And you never get into your Uncle Matt's race car again.

THE END

"Any last words, scum?" says the man who has the tightest grip on your arm.

What's the best way to stall a group of angry, homicidal people? Well, you could try to make them see the lighter side of the situation. You could probably just as likely teach them to fly by flapping their arms, but it's worth a try.

"Tell me this," you say in a shaky voice, "why did the condemned prisoner call for a tailor right before his hanging? Because he was fit to be tied!"

Half the people don't hear you above their own screaming voices. The other half do, but they don't believe what they're hearing.

"How about this one? Two condemned prisoners were having a race to see who would die first. One was going to be hanged; the other was going to be shot. Who won? The prisoner being hanged won by a neck in the stretch. Hahaha — get it?"

They get it. And now most of them are laughing and slapping their knees. Apparently an appreciation for bad jokes is something that hasn't changed much in 70 years. Then someone stands up on a nearby fence and hushes the crowd.

Go on to PAGE 85.

"Wait a minute, everybody — listen to me! This ain't the kid! I talked to that kid; and believe me, that little firebug has a voice that could chill a snowman right to the bones. We've made a big mistake. This ain't the right kid!"

The crowd actually applauds as they untie your hands, legs, arms, and throat. But they don't let you go — not until you tell them 15 or 20 more jokes.

When the show is over, get back in the car and drive over to PAGE 49.

You drive on, your foot and leg numb from the hours of holding down the gas pedal.

Suddenly, a picture flashes in your mind. There was something strange about that last car of the Baron's — the one you passed 60 miles back. The others were hidden off the main road, pointing in the direction of the race. The last one was in a side road, pointing in a different direction.

The finish line flags and banners are in sight now, but you suddenly turn the car around as fast as you can. "The Baron's not going to the finish line!" you shout.

"Neither are you at the moment. Are you crazy?" Corney shouts.

You retrace your route for the 60 miles. But when you get there, Von Furlhoofen's third car is gone. You roar up the bumpy side road in the direction his car had been pointing.

The chase ends at the Monterey marina. Von Furlhoofen is sitting in his racer, parked by the water and watching a small rowboat coming nearer the shore. Farther out in the water is a German submarine!

"Get out of the car!" you shout at Corney. "I've got to stop him from escaping with the secrets, and there's only one way!" you shout as you floor the gas pedal and head straight for the Baron's car.

Catch the full impact of your plan on PAGE 83!

"You're a spy," you say.

The Baron waves his hand at you, as though brushing away a bothersome fly. "I am a loyal soldier to my country, just as your Uncle Max is a loyal soldier to your country. He was getting too close to me and to this secret letter. It was time for me to blow him up," the Baron says, without a trace of regret in his voice.

"Then you're a jerk," you snap.

"A jerk? What's a jerk?" the Baron asks, first you and then the still silent pilot, who shrugs his shoulders. "Tell me what the word means," the Baron says, standing so close to your face that you can smell the pomade in his hair.

If you usually think quickly on your feet, flip to PAGE 35.

If you usually panic under pressure, turn to PAGE 91.

The McDonald twins go one way, following the route of the race, and you and Corney go the other, heading back for the nearest town to try to get some answers.

As you drive into town, people start yelling and pointing at your racer. A man runs out of the bank and comes up to your racer. "Okay, okay. I lied," he says. "I've got a gold tooth." He pulls it out of his mouth and hands it to you. "Take it and leave us alone!"

You and Corney look at each other. "What's that supposed to mean?" you ask.

However, there can be no doubt about the meaning of the revolver in the hands of the tall, thin man wearing a badge. "I'm glad to see that you two had a change of heart and decided to give yourselves up," he says.

"Sheriff, we want to report a robbery," you say, trying to change the subject.

"Very funny. But our bank vice president already reported the robbery. Two masked bandits, driving that racing automobile right there, held up the bank across the street not more than three hours ago."

Eyewitnesses back then aren't what they are today, and neither are trials. But a prison sentence of 20 years is still 20 years. Fortunately, when you get out in 1935, movies will be in color and have sound! It gives you something to look forward to.

THE END

You don't win.

THE END

"It means you don't know anything," you say without thinking. "Every seventh-grader knows that Mexico didn't enter the First World War. And when the United States entered the war in 1917, the war was over within a year. And I'll tell you something else, sucker. You Lost!"

The words come angry and fast. You see that the Baron is staring at you, first without moving, but then coming closer. "How do you know that the war will be over three years from now?" he says, shaking you.

"I, uh, made it up," you say nervously.

"I don't believe you! Tell me how you know these things immediately, or I will kill you!" the Baron says. And you know he's not making *that* up.

You don't want to, but your life depends on telling the Baron that you are from the future. He believes you and unties the ropes. But instead of letting you go, he holds you prisoner, picking your brain for every detail about the future.

Two years later, the Baron goes mad from knowing so much about the world's destiny and not being able to change it. And you escape to live with your Uncle Max again. But you must live the rest of your life with two secrets — who you are and what you have been doing for the last two years.

THE END

You enter the telegraph office, which is also the newspaper office and the hospital and the barbershop. "I want to send a telegram," you say, and you reach into your pocket to get the copy of the message you want to send to Uncle Max. As you do, a nail rips through your hand.

"Let me see your hand," the barber says. "That's quite a cut; I'm going to have to stitch it up for you."

Suddenly you get a great idea!

"Forget the telegram!" you say. "I want to place an ad in the paper."

As fast as you can, you scribble down this message: *I, Jamie Blunt, offer a reward for the capture of my missing identical twin. My twin is a known arsonist who has been impersonating me. You'll know me by a deep cut on my right hand.*

The newspaper prints the ad along with the photo from the WANTED poster. A week later, a Model T drives into town. Sitting next to the driver is the arsonist, tied from head to foot. Uncle Max arrives later to pay the reward and to take you home.

You've still got a lot of choices to make about staying in the past and what to tell Uncle Max and how to live a happy life 70 years ago. But those decisions can wait until tomorrow. Tonight you can sleep peacefully, knowing that no one is chasing you.

THE END

Back in Boston, Corney explains to Uncle Max the secret of where you come from. Then he drives you to a small but pretty cottage. "This is where my friend Gwen lives," he says. "She was the other person who told me she was from the future."

"I can't wait to meet her. Maybe she knows a way out of this time," Matt says.

"Not so fast," Corney says sternly. "If you're from the future, who will be the President of the United States in 1980?"

"Ronald Reagan," you answer.

"Wait here," Corney says. And then he goes to the door, knocks, and enters.

Soon he rushes out. "By gosh! She said the same thing! Come in."

You rush in, and without even a hello, you ask how can you get back to the 1980s.

"Are you sure you want to go?" Gwen asks. "What about the chemicals in the water systems? What about the earthquake that destroyed California?"

"What are you talking about?" you say. "That hasn't happened!"

"It will," Gwen says. "You see, I know about the 1980s from my history classes. I lived in the year 2084. I came back here to escape the unhappiness of my world."

"I'm sorry I doubted you," Corney says. She smiles. You and your Uncle Matt decide to make the best of it in 1915.

THE END

**Collect All Ten Twistaplot™ Books
And Choose From Over 200 Endings!**

#1 *The Time Raider* by R.L. Stine
#2 *The Train of Terror* by Louise Munro Foley
#3 *The Formula for Trouble* by Megan Stine and H. William Stine
#4 *Golden Sword of Dragonwalk* by R.L. Stine
#5 *The Sinister Studios of KESP-TV* by Louise Munro Foley
#6 *Crash Landing* by Arthur Roth
#7 *The Video Avenger* by Douglas Colligan
#8 *Race Into the Past* by Megan Stine and H. William Stine
#9 *Horrors of the Haunted Museum* by R.L. Stine
#10 *Mission of the Secret Spy Squad* by Ruth Glick and Eileen Buckholtz